THE *Little Princesses* SERIES

Little Princesses
The Golden Princess

By Katie Chase

Illustrated by Leighton Noyes

Red Fox

Special thanks to Narinder Dhami

THE GOLDEN PRINCESS
A RED FOX BOOK 978 0 099 48843 9

First published in Great Britain by Red Fox,
an imprint of Random House Children's Books

This edition published 2007

1 3 5 7 9 10 8 6 4 2

Series created by Working Partners Ltd
Copyright © Working Partners Ltd, 2007
Illustrations copyright © Leighton Noyes, 2007
Cover illustration by Nila Aye

Set in 13/21pt Bembo Schoolbook

Red Fox Books are published by Random House Children's Books,
61–63 Uxbridge Road, London W5 5SA,
a division of The Random House Group Limited.
Addresses for companies within The Random House Group Limited can be found at:
www.randomhouse.co.uk/offices.htm

THE RANDOM HOUSE GROUP Limited Reg. No. 954009
www.kidsatrandomhouse.co.uk

A CIP catalogue record for this book is available from the British Library.

Printed and bound in Great Britain by
Bookmarque Ltd, Croydon, Surrey

For Bam and Jam – *W.P.*

For Duncan, Sara and Emma,
with all my thanks – *L.N.*

Chapter One

"Luke! Where are you?"

Rosie hurried into the Great Hall of the castle and looked around, but her brother was nowhere in sight. He was probably playing in his bedroom, she decided. She went over to the wide oak staircase and skipped up the stairs.

It's great living in a castle! Rosie thought happily. I'll never get tired of it!

The castle in the Scottish Highlands belonged to Rosie's favourite relative, Great-aunt Rosamund. Rosie's great-aunt loved to travel the world collecting antiques and treasures for her beautiful home, and she was

away again on another long trip. This time
she'd asked Rosie and her family to move in
and look after the castle while she was gone.
Rosie was thrilled. Every day seemed like a
fairytale when she woke up in her round
bedroom in one of the castle's turrets.

Rosie hurried down the landing and up
the spiral staircase that led to the top of
another turret. Luke's bedroom door was
firmly closed, which Rosie thought was
rather strange. When Luke was playing, he
and his toys usually spilled out of his room
onto the landing.

"Luke!" she called, rapping on the big wooden door. "Mum wants to know if you want a sandwich."

"Oh!" Luke replied, sounding startled and a little bit guilty. "Just a minute, Rosie!"

Rosie frowned and put her ear to the door. She could hear lots of shuffling coming from the other side. He's up to something! she thought, and flung the door open.

Luke was sitting on the floor surrounded by a jumble of toy cars. He almost jumped out of his skin when Rosie marched in. Quickly he scrambled to his feet, biting his lip.

"What's going on?" asked Rosie suspiciously.

"Nothing," Luke muttered. But Rosie noticed that he couldn't look her in the eye.

"OK," she replied with a shrug. "Maybe I'll just go and tell Mum that you don't want a

sandwich because you're too busy doing
something naughty!"

Luke looked even more guilty. "I didn't
mean to do it!" he said anxiously.

"Do what?" Rosie asked.

Slowly Luke knelt down and slid his hand
under the bed to pull out two dazzling pieces
of curved golden metal.

"I found this in my room ages ago," he
explained miserably, handing the metal
pieces to Rosie. "But I accidentally broke it.
I think it's some kind of necklace."

Rosie's eyes opened wide with surprise as she examined the metal. "It is a kind of necklace," she agreed. "It's called a torque. I had to wear one once when we did a play at school about Queen Elizabeth the First. It fits around your neck and sits on your collarbone." She glanced sternly at Luke. "How did you break it?"

"I was using it as a ramp for my toy cars," Luke muttered. "It was great because it's curved and really smooth, but then it snapped and I can't put it back together."

Rosie shook her head. "Luke, you know we have to be really careful with Great-aunt Rosamund's things," she pointed out. "You should have told Mum and Dad that you'd found this."

"I know," Luke sighed. "I'm really sorry."

Rosie weighed the pieces of the torque in her hand. It was so heavy, she was sure it was solid gold. Then she looked more closely at the place where it had snapped. Suddenly a smile spread across her face. "Luke, it isn't broken!" she announced. "Look, it's supposed to come apart so that you can get it on and off more easily!"

"Really?" Luke gasped, his face lighting up with relief.

Rosie nodded. It took her a few minutes, but eventually she managed to slot the two pieces together. There was a snap as they slid into place.

"Brilliant!" Luke exclaimed.

"But no more using it as a car ramp," Rosie said with a grin. "I'll put it in Mum and Dad's room."

"OK," replied Luke, bouncing over to the door with all his usual energy. "I'll go and have my sandwich now."

When Luke had gone, Rosie went down

to her parents' bedroom, carrying the torque
carefully. She put it down on the dressing
table but couldn't tear her eyes away
from the beautiful necklace. It was engraved
with delicate patterns, and at one end she
saw the figure of a sad-
looking girl wearing
a long dress and a
crown. "It's a little
princess!" Rosie
gasped.

Rosie had
learned all about the
little princesses from a secret
letter that Great-aunt Rosamund had left for
her. Now, whenever Rosie discovered one of
the princesses hidden around the castle, a
magical adventure always followed.

She bobbed a curtsey, just as her great-
aunt had told her to. "Hello!" she said softly.

Immediately a gentle breeze swirled through the room. It felt cool and crisp, like mountain air, and it swept Rosie off her feet as flecks of golden dust danced around her and the smell of lush green grass filled her nostrils.

I wonder where I'm going this time, Rosie thought, closing her eyes and remembering all her previous exciting adventures. Seconds later the breeze died away and Rosie felt herself land lightly on the ground.

She opened her eyes and looked around
eagerly to see that she was standing in a
green valley between two mountains, under
a deep blue sky.

THUD!

Rosie jumped as an enormous block of
grey stone crashed down right beside her. It
was so enormous, it made the ground under
her feet tremble. "Oh!" she gasped, leaping
aside. "Where did *that* come from?"

She glanced up and, to her amazement,
saw a huge stone figure, towering above her.

It's a *giant*! Rosie thought, her heart
thumping with terror. And that wasn't just a
block of stone – it was his *foot*!

She gazed up at the giant in awe. He
seemed to be made entirely of dark rock and
there was moss and lichen growing on his
head and chin. His face was angular and his
eyes were deep set. Rosie thought that he

looked sad.
But she had no
time to consider
it because at that
moment the stone
giant lifted his other
foot, and she watched
in horror as it
started to come
down right
over her
head.

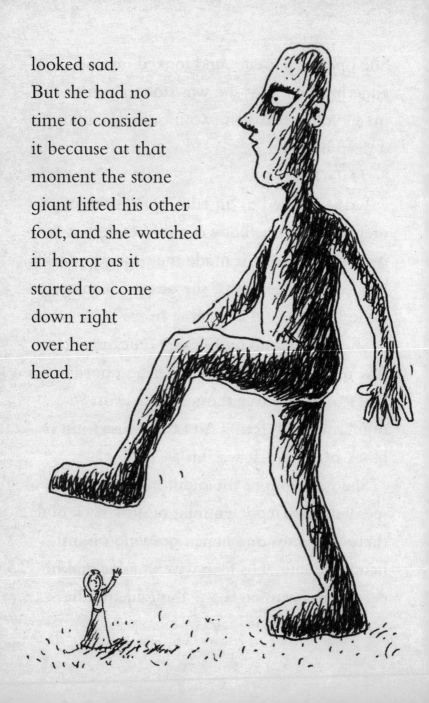

Chapter Two

Frozen with fear, Rosie couldn't jump out of
the way and the giant's foot was only
centimetres from her head when suddenly she
felt someone grab her hand. In the nick of
time she was pulled out from under the
descending stone foot and dragged to safety
in a spinney of trees.

"Oh, thank you!" Rosie gasped, staring at
the girl who'd rescued her.

She had long, shining black hair and
golden-brown skin, and she was richly
dressed in a long-sleeved white robe. For the
first time, Rosie noticed that she herself was
dressed in a similar long-sleeved purple robe.

She also had golden bangles on her arms, but
the girl next to her was wearing far more
magnificent golden jewellery. She had long
golden earrings in her ears, a gold headdress
on her head and wide golden bangles on her
arms. A torque, very much like the one Luke
had been playing with, circled her neck.
Rosie was sure that this was the little
princess.

The girl smiled warmly at Rosie but her eyes were anxious. "Hello, I'm Princess Chayna," she said. "I'm not supposed to be here, so we must keep out of sight," she went on, glancing nervously around.

Rosie smiled at her. "My name's Rosie," she whispered. "Thank you for saving me from being crushed by the giant's foot, but why do you have to hide?"

The girl drew Rosie to the edge of the spinney and pointed out across the valley. Rosie peeped out. To her amazement she could see five more stone giants standing in a row. The sixth giant, the one who had almost put his foot down on top of her, was striding towards them. He was followed by a man wearing a robe of orange and gold, who was followed in turn by a shorter man in a shabby white robe, who looked rather fearful of the giants.

The princess pointed at the man in the orange robe. "I believe that man is tricking my people," she explained. "I've been following him secretly to try and find out what he's up to. That's why he mustn't know I'm here."

The man Chayna had pointed out was now climbing a nearby rocky outcrop. When he reached the top, he waved at the giants.

"Giants!" he called loudly so that the giants could hear him. "I am sad to say that I am very displeased with you!"

"Quizo, esteemed high priest of the Inca people, we are sorry we have displeased you," all six giants said together, their voices deep and rumbling. "We know that we have failed to carry out your orders, but we must talk to you."

Rosie's eyes widened with excitement when she heard the giants mention the Inca people. She didn't know much about the Inca, but she did remember hearing that they were an ancient race who had lived in South America and that they had had fabulous golden treasures!

"Silence!" Quizo snarled, raising his hand. "I will do the talking! Firstly I want to know why I have just found one of you crying into a stream, instead of following my orders!" And he glared at the sixth giant.

The sixth giant looked very sad and not scary at all.

Rosie suddenly felt sorry for him.

"I was crying because I'm so tired!" he sniffled. "We've been stomping and roaring for weeks now. I don't want to do it any more!" And the other giants nodded in agreement, all looking extremely miserable.

Rosie glanced at the little princess, wondering what was going on, but she didn't dare speak in case she was overheard. She wasn't worried about the giants now because the high priest Quizo seemed much nastier. He had a thin, cruel mouth and cold dark eyes.

Quizo sighed loudly. "I will send you to sleep tomorrow!" he snapped. "But until then, you will do as I say and stomp and roar as loudly as you can!"

"But we need a rest," one of the giants said timidly.

Quizo whipped round and glared at him, and they all cowered.

"You will rest very soon, my friends," he said smoothly, looking slightly more friendly. "But remember that your stomping and roaring is all for the sake of the Inca people. As you know, it keeps our enemies away."

The giants nodded guiltily.

"Yes, it is our duty to protect the Inca," the sixth giant agreed.

"And as great Quizo was the one to awaken us from our sleep, we must obey him," another added. There was a loud creaking sound as all the giants bowed their enormous stone heads to the high priest.

"Now, stomp and roar!" Quizo declared, raising his arms in the air. "And keep the Inca safe from harm!"

With an effort, all six giants lifted their feet and brought them crashing down onto the ground. At the same time they all opened their mouths and began to roar loudly.

Rosie had never heard anything like it.
The noise was deafening! The ground
beneath her feet shook like jelly
and even the trees began
swaying. She clapped
her hands over her
ears but it hardly
helped to muffle the din.
Quizo had climbed
down quickly from the rock and he and his
companion were now hurrying away. The
princess beckoned urgently to Rosie, so Rosie
took her hands away from her ears.

"It is just as I suspected," said the little
princess unhappily. "Quizo has been lying.
He has told my people that the stone giants
are sent by our Sun God, Inti, to punish us,
but it's clear that really the giants have been
under Quizo's control all along! I must follow
Quizo and see what else I can learn."

Rosie nodded. "I'll come with you," she said. "You might need some help."

The princess smiled, looking very grateful, and the two girls ran after the men, darting from tree to boulder to avoid being seen. Leaving the green valley, they followed Quizo along the mountainside until eventually the sound of the giants got fainter.

"Please, master, wait for me," the high priest's companion said breathlessly, struggling to keep up.

Quizo turned round and frowned irritably

at the other man but he stopped and waited.
Rosie and Chayna darted quickly behind a
bush and watched.

"That went well, didn't it, Quizo?" panted
the shorter man as he caught up and sank
down on a nearby boulder. "Are you really
going to let the giants sleep tomorrow?"

The priest snorted loudly. "Don't be a
fool, Zope!" he snapped. "The giants are
stupid and will do whatever I say. They don't
realize they are being tricked – and neither
do the Inca!"

Rosie and the princess exchanged a glance. Clearly Rosie's new friend was right about the high priest!

"You're very cunning, master," said Zope admiringly.

Quizo chuckled nastily. "I know," he replied. "My plan to steal our people's treasure is working well!" He rubbed his hands together greedily. "The people are so scared of the giants that they are happy to give me all their precious gold so I can offer it up to the Sun God, Inti. They hope the gold will please him and he will send the giants away!"

"But you are keeping all the gold yourself!" put in Zope. "It's a brilliant plan!

You won't forget my share, though, will you, master? You know I've helped you."

Quizo glared at Zope. "I didn't need any help," the high priest said imperiously. "I'm so clever that the rest of the Inca and the giants will never work out what is going on!"

Chapter Three

What a horrid man! Rosie thought. She took the princess's hand and gave it a sympathetic squeeze and the princess smiled gratefully at her.

"Today we celebrate the Festival of the Sun," Quizo went on. "You may rest here for a few minutes more but then we must go on, for soon the Temple of Inti will be filled with gold coins – and we have to be there to steal them!"

Zope nodded. "What's your plan when the festival is finished, master?" he asked, mopping his brow.

Rosie and the princess leaned forward as far as they could, anxious to hear Quizo's reply.

"Once we have gathered all the coins from the temple, we will take the rest of the treasure and leave as quickly as we can," Quizo told him.

"But the people will come after us when they find we've left with all the gold," Zope pointed out nervously.

"Do you think I haven't thought of that?" scowled Quizo. "We shall visit the giants one last time and trick them into stomping all over the city!

That way the people will be too busy
rebuilding their homes to come after us –
if they even survive!"

Zope laughed. "Master, you are a genius!"
he said. "But what about the king? He's not
so stupid and neither is the Princess Chayna.
In fact, she's always snooping about and
spying!"

The princess smiled at Rosie and Rosie
grinned back.

"And we'll have to be careful when
everyone comes to the Temple of Inti for
the festival," Zope went on, "because if
anyone were to find the spell that will send
the giants back to sleep, everything would
be ruined."

"Idiot!" roared Quizo furiously. "Keep your
voice down!" And he whipped round quickly
to scan his surroundings.

Rosie and the princess swiftly drew back

behind the bush.
Rosie felt icy cold
with fear. Had
Quizo spotted
them? For a
moment or two
he gazed at the
mountains as Rosie and
Chayna held their breath.

"I'm sorry, master," Zope
muttered as Quizo finally relaxed and turned
back to his companion.

"Just be more careful in future!" Quizo
snapped. "Anyway, no one's going to find the
spell. It's in a very safe place."

Zope stared eagerly at Quizo. "Where,
master?"

Quizo lowered his voice and Rosie strained
her ears to hear what he said. "The spell is
exactly where I found it," he murmured.

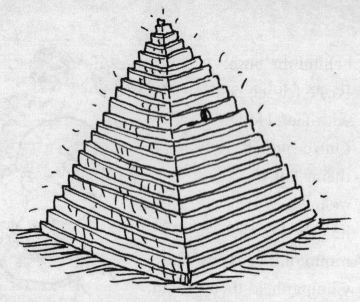

"In the secret chamber at the heart of the Temple of Inti!"

Zope grinned. "An excellent idea, master," he said. "Nobody will be able to reach it because of all the ancient traps you told me about."

"True." Quizo puffed out his chest, looking like a very proud peacock. "It took *me* months to find my way to the secret chamber and find the spell that wakes the giants, and the spell that sends them back to sleep. I only managed it because I'm so extraordinarily clever! Nobody else stands a chance." He glanced up at the sun in the sky. "Come, Zope, we must walk on. Time is short."

Rosie and the princess waited until Zope and Quizo were out of sight.

Then the princess turned to Rosie. "You see what a terrible man Quizo is?" she asked, frowning angrily.

Rosie nodded and the princess sighed. Then she brightened.

"You must be very brave, Rosie, because you didn't even scream when you saw the stone giants!" Chayna said, her dark eyes twinkling.

"Well, I was scared but I've seen some pretty amazing things in the last few months," Rosie explained. "I came here by magic, Chayna! My Great-aunt Rosamund told me how."

Chayna looked thrilled. "*My* great-aunt used to tell me about her magical friend called

Rosamund who came from the future!" she cried. "Rosamund and my great-aunt used to have lots of fun together. You must be *my* magic friend, Rosie!" But then Chayna's face fell and she sighed. "We won't be having lots of fun, though, unfortunately.
I have to decide what to do about Quizo."

"Yes, I heard everything he said," Rosie replied, feeling angry.

Chayna nodded. "My people have been living in fear of the giants for weeks," she sighed. "They first appeared over a month ago and Quizo said it was because our Sun God, Inti, was angry with us. Quizo claims that only his prayers and incantations are keeping the giants from crushing our city. He says the people must give all their treasures to Inti to please him and make him send the giants away. But it is all a trick so that Quizo can get the treasure for himself. I *must* think of a way to stop his evil plan."

Rosie nodded. "I'll help you!" she declared.

Chapter Four

"Thank you, Rosie," Chayna replied, beaming at her new friend. "Now we must go to the City of Gold so that I can tell my father what Quizo is up to. He cannot be allowed to destroy our beautiful city, or steal all the gold that my people are offering to Inti!"

"We'd better hurry," Rosie said urgently. "Didn't Quizo say he was going to leave with all the gold after the Festival of the Sun today?"

Chayna nodded. "This way," she said, pointing to a winding

mountain track. "If we take this route, there's no danger that we'll bump into Quizo and Zope."

The two girls set off at a brisk pace. The sun was steadily climbing in the blue sky and Rosie and Chayna knew that they couldn't afford to waste time. Rosie's legs began to ache as the two of them climbed higher and

higher. She was feeling very thirsty too, so she was glad when Chayna stopped and unclipped a gold flask from her belt.

"Would you like a drink of water, Rosie?" Chayna asked, holding the flask out.

Rosie nodded gratefully. The water was cool and tasted delicious. "That's lovely," she sighed, handing the flask back to Chayna.

"It's fresh water from one of the mountain streams," Chayna explained, taking a drink herself. "See how high up we are?"

Rosie hadn't realized quite how far they had climbed. But now she could see that the valley they had reached overlooked other green valleys and shining lakes far below them. In the distance she could see the sea and the outline of an island on the horizon.

The girls carried on upwards, and Rosie saw that they were now as high as the clouds.

Then Chayna paused. "This way, Rosie," she said and, stepping forwards towards the rock face, she suddenly disappeared.

Rosie stared in amazement. Where had her friend gone? Then she saw that two huge overlapping rocks hid the narrow entrance to a rocky mountain pass. She slipped through the opening after Chayna.

The mountain pass led to a beautiful leafy valley, nestled between two enormous mountains whose peaks were wreathed in mist. The grass was lush and green, trees laden with fruit grew here and there and colourful

birds soared overhead in the blue sky.

"This is gorgeous!" Rosie breathed. Then
she spotted a group of animals with long,
shaggy white coats grazing peacefully on the
green grass. "What are they?"

"They're llamas," Chayna replied. "We use
the hair from their long coats to weave
cloth." She smiled at Rosie, who was still
staring at the llamas in fascination. "It's not
too far now but the track does get much
steeper."

The girls hurried on and soon Rosie found
herself scrambling up a steep, rocky incline.
She could see a beautiful golden glow ahead
of her. "What's that?" she asked breathlessly.

Chayna laughed. "That's the City of
Gold!" she announced.

When they reached the top of the incline,
Rosie gazed eagerly down into the green
valley beyond and let out a gasp. There,

spread out before her and glittering in the
bright sunshine, was the City of Gold. She
could see that it was made up of white stone
buildings with roofs of shining gold. The sun
glinted off the dazzling golden rooftops,
creating a burnished glow that filled the
whole city. Rosie had never seen anything
so dazzling.

"It's the most beautiful city I've ever seen!"
she cried.

Chayna smiled proudly. "The Inca are the

children of the sun," she told Rosie. "That is
why gold is so important to us."

The girls scrambled down the rocky
mountainside towards a huge golden arch
which marked the entrance to the city.
As the girls walked through it, Rosie noticed
a magnificent step pyramid, also covered in
gold, which shone almost as brightly as the
sun itself.

"That is the Temple of Inti," Chayna told
her.

All the way up the steps at the front of the temple, Rosie could see heaps of glittering jewels, as well as goblets, plates, bowls and other objects made of gold. There were people queuing to place still more treasure on the piles, and Rosie realized that these were the offerings the Inca were making to Inti the Sun God – the treasure that Quizo was planning to steal!

Although the girls were now a long way from the giants' valley, the stomping and roaring of the stone giants could still be heard echoing faintly around the city.

Rosie noticed that several of the people were looking fearfully into the distance.

Chayna frowned. "We must hurry and tell my father about Quizo, Rosie," she said in a low voice. "The palace is not far from here."

But when they reached the royal palace, the king was already on his way out. A huge procession of people was waiting for him in the courtyard, with Quizo at its head. When the king saw the girls, he hurried over, looking cross. Rosie watched him approach and noticed that he had dark hair and eyes like Chayna's, and a small neat beard. He wore a gold circlet on his head and his robe was purple, edged with gold.

"Chayna! Where have you been and who is this?" the king demanded, looking at Rosie.

"I'm sorry, Father," Chayna replied. "This is Rosie, my new friend, and—"

The king interrupted. "I'm very pleased to meet you, Rosie," he said kindly. "You are most welcome to the land of the Inca. But now I must ask you both to join the back of the procession and accompany us to the temple immediately. The Festival of the Sun is about to begin. We must not further annoy our beloved Sun God by being late."

"But, Fa—" Chayna began. But the king was already hurrying away to take his place next to Quizo at the head of the people.

"Well!" Chayna exclaimed as she and Rosie walked over to join the end of the procession, which was now heading off towards the temple. "I can't talk to my father now, not while he is standing right next to Quizo!"

"Maybe we can try again later," Rosie suggested.

But Chayna shook her head. "We don't have time," she said. "I can only think of one thing to do. I'm going to have to search the Temple of Inti and find the spell to send the stone giants to sleep myself!"

Rosie nodded. "But not all by yourself," she said. "I'm coming too."

"Thank you, Rosie," Chayna replied

gratefully. "I knew you'd help, but we'll have to be careful. It will be very dangerous, especially if Quizo finds out what we're up to!"

Chapter Five

"I'm not scared," Rosie said bravely. "We must save the City of Gold and stop Quizo getting away with the treasure! But do you know where to find the secret chamber at the heart of the temple, where Quizo said the spell is?"

"No, I don't," Chayna said thoughtfully. "But I *do* know of a secret door in the main temple chamber and the festival celebrations will be taking place in there, so we can use the secret door to slip away during the ceremony."

"Where does it lead?" Rosie asked curiously.

"I've never had a chance to look," Chayna sighed. "There are always priests about. But I'm sure it leads to something interesting, otherwise it wouldn't be secret, right?"

"Right!" Rosie agreed, with a grin. "We'll just have to do some exploring."

At that point, the procession came within sight of the temple and Rosie caught her breath in wonder. It seemed as if everyone in the city had gathered around the glittering golden temple, all dressed in their best clothes and adorned with shining golden jewellery.

The king and Quizo started to climb the stone steps to the temple doors. Rosie could see them talking animatedly as they led the procession. The king laughed at something the high priest said.

Frowning, Chayna turned to Rosie. "My father thinks the high priest is a loyal

subject," she said in a low voice. "He believes
Quizo when he says that only gold and
treasure will please Inti so that our god will
keep the giants from destroying our city.
We *must* find that spell to send the giants
to sleep and show my father that
Quizo has been lying!"

Rosie and Chayna hurried
up the steps of the temple,

between the piles of gold and jewels that Rosie had noticed earlier. Rosie ducked through the wide doorway at the top of the steps, eager to see inside the Temple of Inti.

She hadn't thought it was possible, but the inside of the temple was even more beautiful than the outside! Tall, slender columns, their bases decorated with gold leaf, rose up to support a high roof with a large round hole in the middle, through which the sunlight streamed in. The walls were lined with golden panels engraved with pictures.

"They tell stories of Inti," Chayna explained to Rosie as she noticed her friend staring at the panels. "Come, we must join the others around the sun."

In the middle of the floor there was an enormous painted sun. Everyone was standing around it and looking expectantly

at Quizo, who was next to the king. The priest closed his eyes and began to chant.

As Quizo chanted, the king held up a shining gold coin. Then he threw it down onto the centre of the sun, closed his eyes and began to chant along with Quizo. Chayna pressed a coin into Rosie's hand and when everyone else threw their coins to the ground, Rosie did too. Then the people closed their eyes and began to chant loudly, along with the king and the high priest.

"Everyone has their eyes closed," Chayna whispered to Rosie. "We can sneak away now without being seen!"

Rosie nodded, and she and Chayna

stepped quietly away from the painted sun. She couldn't help glancing nervously at Quizo to see if he was watching them, but the priest's eyes remained firmly closed.

Quickly Chayna led Rosie to the back of the temple chamber. "The door's here," she said, pointing at the gold panel that was etched with a waterfall scene.

Rosie blinked hard and stared at the panel. She couldn't see a door at all!

Chayna grinned at her. "It is a *secret* door!" she whispered. She reached out and touched one of the corners of the panel. Immediately, it slid smoothly aside.

Rosie peered into a dark corridor on the other side. A few burning torches slotted into the wall near the doorway provided the only light.

"We must hurry," Chayna said urgently, stepping through the opening. Rosie followed and quickly helped Chayna to close the panel behind them.

Then Rosie lifted a burning torch off the wall. "We'll need this to find our way through the darkness," she began, but her words were almost drowned out by a loud rumbling sound that echoed deafeningly around the corridor.

"What's that?" Chayna gasped.

Rosie felt the ground shaking and she glanced down.

To her horror, she saw a large chasm opening up in the floor in front of them. As she and Chayna watched, the chasm grew steadily wider and closer to where they were standing.

"Oh, no!" Rosie cried. "The ground's disappearing from beneath our feet!"

Chapter Six

Just in time, Rosie and Chayna managed to jump back, away from the ever-widening rift. Chayna was so scared she accidentally bumped into Rosie, knocking the torch from her hand. It tumbled into the abyss and vanished into the darkness long before they heard it hit the bottom. Rosie's heart pounded with fear as she realized how deep the chasm must be.

"The torch must have been booby-trapped so that when it was moved, it triggered the chasm to open!" Rosie exclaimed. "Now we'll have to jump across to the other side of the chasm before the gap gets any bigger."

She grabbed Chayna's hand. "After three: one, two, *three!*"

Together the girls ran towards the deep black hole and leaped desperately towards the other side. To Rosie's relief, they made it safely across the yawning chasm.

"That was close!" she sighed, shaking her head.

"We'd better be careful from now on," Chayna agreed solemnly. "Anything in here might be a boobytrap!"

The girls set off down the narrow, winding
tunnel. The walls were lined with more
golden panels engraved with pictures. Rosie
saw a mountain scene, a llama, a flower and
one engraving of the Temple of Inti itself.
Although Rosie and Chayna knew they
had to hurry, they kept a sharp look out for
anything that might be dangerous. Luckily
there were more torches on the walls to light
their way, though the girls didn't dare remove
one in case it set off another trap.

"How do we know this is the right way?"
asked Rosie as they passed other smaller
tunnels branching off from the main one.

"Well, this tunnel is sloping down towards the heart of the temple," Chayna replied. "And that's where Quizo said the secret chamber is."

Suddenly something on the ground caught Rosie's eye. "Look, Chayna – footprints!" she said, pointing.

"Do you think they're Quizo's?" asked Chayna.

"Probably," Rosie said excitedly. "I'm sure we're on the right track now, Chayna!"

The two girls walked on eagerly, but all of a sudden they came to a fork in the main corridor.

Chayna frowned. "Which way shall we go?" she asked. Then she brightened. "Oh, of course, we'll follow Quizo's footprints!

They go down the right-hand fork." And, with that, she hurried forward.

But Rosie followed a little more slowly, peering down at the footprints that led into the right-hand fork. Somehow they looked deeper and clearer than the previous ones. It's almost as if somebody's trying to lay a false trail, Rosie thought . . .

"Chayna!" Rosie cried, grabbing her friend's arm. "Wait! I think this might be another trap!"

As Chayna stared at her in amazement, Rosie picked up a rock and threw it into the right-hand tunnel. Immediately a volley of sharp-looking spears shot from one side of the passage to the other. The tips embedded themselves in the opposite wall, the shafts of the spears quivering from the force of the impact.

"Oh!" Chayna gasped, turning quite pale.

"Thank you, Rosie!"

"We'd better take the left-hand fork,"
Rosie said, feeling rather nervous herself.

Chayna looked puzzled. "But, Rosie,
I don't see how Quizo could have gone that
way because there are no footprints!" she
pointed out. "Do you think it could be
another trap?"

Rosie looked carefully at the left-hand
tunnel and noticed something different about
the walls. "Look at the walls!" she exclaimed.
"There are handholds and footholds carved

into them. Quizo must have *climbed* along the tunnel – that's why there aren't any footprints!"

"Then we'll do the same," Chayna replied firmly.

Carefully Rosie placed her foot in the first foothold and then reached for the nearest handhold. Chayna followed her and slowly the girls climbed along the tunnel like mountaineers.

"The footprints start again here," Chayna pointed out, after they'd been going for a little while. "Do you think we can get down now and walk?"

Rosie nodded, and she and Chayna jumped down and continued along the floor of the tunnel. But suddenly they rounded a corner and found themselves staring at a dead end! A wall of stone blocks completely barred the way.

"Oh, no!" Chayna said in dismay. "This must be the wrong way after all!"

"But we can't go back and search *all* the other corridors!" Rosie gasped. "We don't have enough time."

The two girls stared miserably at the wall. But then Rosie noticed something curious. "Look, Chayna!" she said, crouching down and pointing at the ground. "The footprints go right up to the wall. In fact, they seem to

carry on underneath the wall as well – as
if the wall wasn't there when the footprints
were made!"

"So you think Quizo managed to find a
way past!" Chayna cried.

Rosie nodded. "And if he did, we can too!"
she said determinedly. "Maybe there's a secret
lever or something that opens a door."

Hoping the wall wasn't booby-trapped, the
girls began to feel along it for some sort of
mechanism. But they couldn't find anything.

"There must be something," Rosie
murmured, running her fingers lightly over

the surface of the stone blocks. "Quizo thinks he's super-clever, but even *he* can't walk through solid stone!"

Just at that moment, Rosie suddenly felt something strange beneath her fingertips. Quickly she ran her hands over the stones in the centre of the wall again. Twelve of the blocks were very slightly sticking out from the wall, so slightly that it was impossible to tell just by looking.

Rosie examined these blocks more closely and saw that each one had a picture carved on it. One of them showed a waterfall that looked exactly the same as the engraving on the panel on the secret door in the main temple chamber.

"Chayna, look at this," Rosie said, pointing at the carving. "It's the same as the one on the secret door. Do you think it could mean something?"

Chayna took a closer look. "You're right!" she exclaimed. "And these other carvings are the same as some of the pictures we saw along the way." She pointed at a mountain scene and a llama. "I remember both of these!"

"Maybe they're clues!" Rosie suggested, looking excited. Hesitantly she reached out and pushed the waterfall block. It slid smoothly inwards and the two girls glanced at each other in delight.

"The blocks must be some sort of code to open the door!" cried Chayna.

"Do you think we should press the blocks in the order we saw the pictures?" Rosie suggested.

Chayna nodded. "Good idea," she agreed. "And if that doesn't work, we can try something else."

"What was the first picture in the tunnel after the waterfall?" asked Rosie.

"The mountain!"
Chayna replied confidently,
pushing the block in. "And
then I think it was a flower."

"No." Rosie put out her hand to
stop Chayna, who was about to touch the
flower-engraved block. "It was the llama,
then the flower."

Between them the girls worked their way
through the pictures. When all the blocks
except two had been pressed, Rosie frowned
and pointed at an engraving of a tree.

"I don't remember this one," she said.

"I don't remember it, either," agreed
Chayna. "I think it might be another trap,
Rosie!"

"Let's ignore it then," Rosie said.

Chayna nodded and pushed the other
block, which was a picture of the Temple of
Inti. Then the two girls stepped back and

looked at the wall expectantly.

"Nothing!" Chayna said disappointedly. "Do you think the tree fitted in somewhere?"

"Wait," Rosie said, still staring thoughtfully at the pictures. "The wall's moving!"

Sure enough, the wall was sliding smoothly to one side. Chayna and Rosie beamed at each other and then peered cautiously through the opening.

They saw a beautiful but empty circular chamber. It had a high roof with a sun painted in the middle of the ceiling, just like the one on the floor of the main temple chamber.

"Look at this, Rosie!" breathed Chayna as they walked inside. "We're in the very heart of the temple." She pointed up at the sun painted on the ceiling. "This *must* be the secret chamber that Quizo mentioned!"

"We'd better start looking for the spell," Rosie replied eagerly. "I wonder where it could be."

The two girls began to walk around the chamber, scanning every nook and cranny for the spell. As they searched, Rosie's gaze was drawn to an unusual spiral pattern on the floor. The spiral was made up of a gold line and a silver line, running parallel to each other. The glittering lines wound round and round into the very centre of the room, like a snail shell.

Rosie was staring at the floor when she suddenly noticed some strange symbols around the edge. She took a closer look and realized that she could read them. "Chayna!" she called. "There's writing on the floor here!"

Chayna rushed over to join her. "*Where the sweat of the sun meets the tears of the moon, the thirst for what you seek will be quenched,*" Chayna read. Then she smiled. "Well, I understand the first part of the riddle," she said. "According to Inca beliefs, gold is the sweat of the sun and silver is the tears of the moon."

Rosie looked back at the floor. "It must mean these two lines," she said thoughtfully, pointing at the spiral of gold and silver. "Let's follow them and see where they meet. Maybe that's where we'll find the spell!"

The girls very carefully began to follow the parallel lines round and round into the very middle of the room, to the place where the two lines finally met in a tightly coiled disc of silver and gold. The disc was very large – about two metres across.

"But there's nothing here!" Chayna said sadly.

Rosie nodded glumly. Chayna was right. The spell clearly wasn't there. Maybe the mysterious words meant something else . . .

Rosie stared thoughtfully at the floor, while Chayna unscrewed her flask to take a drink. She couldn't take her eyes off the silver and gold spiral and she suddenly noticed that between the gold and silver lines was a narrow, shallow channel.

"Would you like a drink, Rosie?" Chayna asked, holding out the flask.

Rosie looked up and realized that she was, in fact, quite thirsty. *And water quenches your thirst . . .* she thought excitedly. "Oh!" she cried, her face lighting up. "Water!" She jumped up and down in excitement and pointed at Chayna's flask. "Water is the key to solving the riddle!"

Chapter Seven

Chayna looked at Rosie in bewilderment.

"I think we should pour the water into the channel and see what happens!" Rosie explained.

Chayna clapped a hand to her mouth in amazement. "You *are* clever, Rosie!" she said. "I'd never have thought of that!"

Immediately Chayna ran to the beginning of the channel at the edge of the room and tipped up her flask, emptying it completely. The girls watched as the water began to flow down the spiral channel and towards the disc in the middle of the floor.

"Look!" Chayna cried, clutching Rosie's

arm. "The water's disappearing when it reaches the centre of the spiral!"

Rosie nodded and held her breath as the last drops of water disappeared. Chayna was still clutching her arm and both girls stood frozen to the spot, watching and waiting.

Nothing happened.

"Oh dear," Rosie sighed. "Maybe that wasn't the right answer after all."

"No, listen," Chayna whispered. "I can hear something."

A low rumbling noise was coming from the ground beneath their feet. Suddenly the floor began to vibrate. Rosie and Chayna drew back against the wall, worried that the ground might crack down the middle again, as it had done at the start of the tunnel. But something very different was happening.

The whole spiral began to shimmer with

light and the gold and silver disc in the middle of the floor slid back. Then a stone platform started to rise slowly up out of the hole, and sitting in the middle of it was a golden casket.

"The spell must be inside that casket!" Chayna said, breathless with excitement.

"But it doesn't look as if the platform is going to stop," Rosie pointed out as it continued to rise. "We'd better jump on before it's out of reach!"

The girls hurried across the room. Keeping her eyes on the moving platform, Rosie took a cautious leap and landed on it safely. Chayna followed, but she misjudged her jump slightly and lost her balance.

"Chayna!" Rosie yelled, lunging forwards just in time to grab her friend's arm as Chayna slipped from the platform.

"Thanks!" Chayna gasped as Rosie helped her up onto the plinth. "That was a bit too close. Now, Rosie, open the casket; my hands are still trembling."

Slowly Rosie lifted the lid of the gold box. She was very cautious in case it was booby-trapped, but to her relief, nothing happened. Inside was a yellowing scroll, which Rosie handed to Chayna.

Eagerly Chayna unrolled the parchment and scanned the writing. "This is it!" she announced, her eyes shining. "This parchment says that the giants were left here to give protection to the Inca in times of need. The giants were left sleeping, but the spell to wake them and the spell to send them to sleep again are both written here. Whoever wakes the giants controls them; that's why the giants have been obeying Quizo. We did it, Rosie! We found the spell!"

The girls hugged each other and then Chayna rolled the parchment up again.

"Now all we have to do is take this to my father and then the giants can be sent back to sleep until they're *really* needed," Chayna said happily. "But how shall we get down, Rosie?"

Rosie looked over the edge. They were now too high to jump off, and the platform was still rising steadily. "There must be a button or a lever to stop this platform," she replied. "But we'd better find it quickly. We can't jump and we're getting higher all the time!"

Rosie and the princess scoured the stone platform, but they soon realized that there was no way to stop it. And now the platform wasn't far from the painted stone ceiling!

"We can't get off!" Rosie gasped, looking around frantically and wondering what they could do.

"Look, Rosie!" Chayna pointed up at the roof.

"There are some words written around the painted sun. Maybe they will give us a clue to stop the platform."

"I hope so," Rosie said anxiously, "because if we can't stop it, we're going to get squashed!"

Chayna stared eagerly up at the writing. "*The Sun God smiles on you*," she read, as soon as she was close enough.

Rosie's heart sank. The painted sun had a face and it was indeed smiling at them, but that was no help at all.

"Lie down, Chayna!" she gasped, as the platform drew closer to the roof. Heart hammering, Rosie lay down beside her

friend and closed her eyes. All they could do was hope that the platform would stop automatically before it crushed them against the ceiling.

Chapter Eight

Rosie was so scared she could hardly breathe. She could already feel the roof pressing lightly on her back and the platform was still rising . . .

But then the girls heard a noise above them. Rosie twisted her head so that she could see upwards. A panel in the roof, in the middle of the sun's face, was sliding back and the platform was rising up through the hole!

"We're safe, Rosie!" Chayna said in a shaky voice.

The girls sat up and hugged each other. Then, as the platform rose right up through the hole, Rosie and Chayna were amazed to

see piles of glittering gold coins surrounding
them, and the king, Quizo and everyone else
staring at them in complete amazement.

We're back in the main temple chamber! Rosie thought, feeling very relieved, and she couldn't help glancing at Quizo, who looked extremely angry. The platform finally shuddered to a halt but everyone was still too stunned to speak.

As they all stared at the girls, golden sunshine suddenly poured in through the hole in the temple roof. It illuminated every corner, reflecting off the golden surfaces and dazzling them all with its warmth and brightness. Rosie guessed that this was the most important part of the festival, when the sun was at its highest position in the sky and could shine right into the temple.

Meanwhile Quizo had spotted the scroll in Chayna's hand. Red with fury, he darted forward and tried to grab it from her. But Chayna was too quick for him. Holding the scroll tightly in one hand, she took Rosie's hand with the other and dragged her friend away from the priest and the platform.

The king looked from Chayna and Rosie to Quizo, his face puzzled. "What is going on?" he asked in a bewildered voice.

"Father, Rosie and I have found the spell that will put the stone giants back to sleep!" Chayna explained, stepping forward to show her father the scroll.

Quizo scowled and tried to edge his way out of the circle, but people hemmed him in on all sides as they pressed forward to see the spell.

"It's not the stone giants we should fear — it's Quizo!" Chayna continued. "He woke the giants in the first place and tricked them into stomping and roaring. Then he convinced everyone in the city that the giants were sent by Inti and tricked us all into giving him our gold!"

There was an angry murmur from the assembled crowd.

"And after the festival, he was going to run off with all the gold and order the giants to destroy the city!" Rosie added.

The murmuring grew louder.

With a thunderous expression, the king turned to Quizo. "Is this true?" he demanded.

"Of course not, Highness!" Quizo blustered. "How can you think it of me? I, who have always been your loyal servant!"

"It *is* true!"
Chayna cried.
"His servant
Zope knows all
about it!" And she
pointed at Zope, who was trying to sneak
out of the temple unobserved.

Immediately Zope was pushed back
towards the king by some of the angry crowd.

"Have mercy, Highness!" Zope whined, his
face pale. "I didn't want to help Quizo in his
evil plan. He *made* me do it!"

"Silence, you fool!" Quizo roared.

The king stared coldly at the high priest.
"So it *is* true!" he snapped. "For weeks you
have kept the stone giants stomping and
roaring. For weeks my people have feared

for their lives. Guards!" The king raised his hand and some of his men immediately stepped forward. "Quizo and Zope are under arrest – make sure they do not escape!" Then he turned to the crowd. "We will go to see the stone giants and make our peace with them!" the king announced, and everyone began to make their way out of the temple.

The king turned to beam at Rosie and Chayna. "My daughter," he said, embracing the princess, "you and your friend have done very well!"

Rosie and Chayna smiled happily at each other. Then they set off with the king to the valley of the stone giants.

Word of Quizo's deception had spread quickly, and many people came to join the crowd. By the time they reached the edge of the valley, there were hundreds of people. The giants were still stomping and roaring, so everyone had their hands over their ears.

When the giants saw the huge crowd approaching, they looked puzzled.

Then they spotted Quizo in the custody of the king's guards and their expressions became hostile. They glared at the crowd and Rosie felt her heart miss a beat. The giants obviously still thought Quizo was their friend and they didn't like to see him a prisoner. What if the giants wouldn't listen to them?

Chapter Nine

Chayna grabbed Rosie's hand and, before
the king could stop them, they climbed up
the rocky outcrop to face the angry giants.

"We have the spell to send you back to
sleep!" Rosie and Chayna shouted together
as loudly as they could.

The giants looked at each other and
finally stopped their stomping and roaring.
The people below took their hands away
from their ears in relief.

"*What* did you say?" one of the giants
asked hopefully. "I *thought* you said you had
the spell to send us back to sleep!"

Chayna nodded and waved the scroll.

"Here it is!" she said.

The giants still looked a little suspicious.

"But why is Quizo under arrest?" one of them asked. "He awakened us to guard the Inca from their enemies."

"There are no enemies!" Chayna assured them. "It was all an evil plan thought up by Quizo."

"He wanted to steal the Inca's gold," Rosie explained. "So he told them that they must offer it to the Sun God to keep them safe from *you!*"

The giants glowered at Quizo, who stared back sullenly.

"Giants, we wish to make our peace with you," the king put in, climbing the rocky outcrop. "Thank you for trying to protect the Inca. Now, please help us to punish Quizo and his manservant, Zope, as they deserve!"

There was a loud grinding sound as the giants nodded their stone heads.

"Take them far, far away from the land of the Inca!" the king commanded, and everyone cheered.

The sixth giant, the one who had almost stepped on Rosie, picked up Quizo in one hand and Zope in the other, and strode off towards the sea. His enormous steps covered the distance in no time and he was soon wading into the water. Rosie and Chayna watched wide-eyed as the giant strode towards the island on the horizon, deposited Quizo and Zope on the ground, and then walked back to the people gathered in the valley.

"I left them on that island far away," the giant explained. "They will never bother the Inca again!"

The crowd cheered and the giant looked rather pleased with himself. He smiled shyly down at them all.

"May we go back to sleep then, Highness?" asked one of the other giants.

The king nodded, and the giants' huge stone faces were filled with joy.

"And rest assured, my friends, that I will keep the spell safely under lock and key," the king added firmly. "We will only wake you again if we are ever in real danger."

He said something to Chayna in a low voice and she beamed at him. Then she handed the scroll to Rosie.

"Rosie, we would be honoured if you'd read the spell," she said, "because without your help, I'd never have found it!"

Rosie blushed as everyone cheered again. She opened the scroll and scanned it quickly, looking for the spell to let the giants sleep. Then, taking a deep breath, she read the spell aloud:

"Now your work is over and done,
Lay your heads down one by one,
Sleep in peace, and soundly too,
Until the Inca call for you!"

The giants sighed
happily and stretched
their huge stone
arms up to the
sky. Then they
each yawned
loudly, one by
one, lay gently
down on the ground
and curled themselves up
comfortably. Rosie watched
in amazement as their features
gradually began to blur and soften
until, finally, they looked just like

six huge boulders standing in a row.

The king clapped his hands. "We must celebrate!" he announced with a smile. "Let us return to the City of Gold and finish our Festival of the Sun properly!"

There were more cheers, and Chayna took Rosie's hand.

"You'll stay for the celebrations, won't you, Rosie?" she asked.

"I'd love to!" Rosie laughed.

"You and my beloved daughter have saved us all!" the king said, putting one arm round Rosie's shoulders and the other round

Chayna's. "The Inca cannot thank you enough!"

The sun was shining down on the City of Gold when the people returned. The king ordered tables to be set up around the Temple of Inti and soon the palace kitchens were busy turning out dish after dish of delicious food.

Everyone danced and sang and Rosie had a wonderful time until, at last, she knew it was time for her to leave.

"Rosie, I shall miss you so much!" Chayna declared, giving her a hug. "Thank you for all your help and promise to come back soon."

"Definitely. I promise," Rosie said, smiling at Chayna and waving at everyone. "Goodbye!"

Immediately the warm scented breeze swept Rosie up and whisked her off home again. The last thing she saw before she closed her eyes was the shining roofs of the City of Gold.

Then, suddenly, her feet touched the ground again and she opened her eyes as the breeze drifted away. She was back in her parents' bedroom, looking at the torque. And now the princess engraved on the necklace looked smiling and happy.

Rosie grinned. I wonder what Luke would say if he knew that this torque actually took me to the land of the Inca, she thought. I don't suppose he'd be using it as a car ramp!

She stared down at the gold, remembering
her exciting adventure.

"Rosie! *Rosie!*"

Gradually Rosie realized that Luke was
calling her name. She blinked and looked
up to see him standing in the doorway,
holding a plate with a sandwich on it.

"I've brought you a sandwich," he said, "but if you don't want it, *I'll* eat it!" And he ran off laughing.

"Give me that!" Rosie shouted. And, laughing too, she dashed after her brother.

THE END

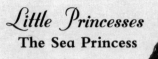

Little Princesses
The Sea Princess

Katie Chase

Rosie knows a very special secret.
Hidden in her great-aunt's mysterious
Scottish castle are lots of little princesses
for her to find. And each one will
whisk her away to another part of the
world on a magical adventure!

Marissa, the Sea Princess, needs Rosie's help
to find her crown and the Pearl of Wisdom
that will restore order to the underwater kingdom
of Aquatica. However, to find it, the girls must
swim down to the bottom of the ocean and
enter the cave of the Sea Hag.

Join Rosie and meet her exciting new friends,
as she discovers all the Little Princesses.

978 0 099 48842 2

www.kidsatrandomhouse.co.uk/littleprincesses

Little Princesses
The Rain Princess

Katie Chase

Rosie knows a very special secret. Hidden in her great-aunt's mysterious Scottish castle are lots of little princesses for her to find. And each one will whisk her away to another part of the world on a magical adventure!

Imena, the Rain Princess, can't make the rains come, however hard she tries. The river will soon be dry and Imena's tribe is running out of time. But one night Rosie and Imena sneak out of the village to try and discover the real reason for the drought.

Join Rosie and meet her exciting new friends, as she discovers all the Little Princesses.

978 0 099 48833 0

www.kidsatrandomhouse.co.uk/littleprincesses

Little Princesses
The Dream-catcher Princess

Katie Chase

Rosie knows a very special secret.
Hidden in her great-aunt's
mysterious Scottish castle
are lots of little princesses
for her to find. And each
one will whisk her away
to another part of the
world on a magical adventure!

Malila, the Dream-catcher Princess, has to
save her people from the monsters of
the Shadow Lands who hunt after dark!
She sets out with Rosie to find the tribe's
mystical dream-catcher, but the girls
must be back before nightfall . . .

Join Rosie and meet her exciting new
friends, as she discovers all
the Little Princesses.

978 0 099 48835 4

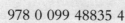

www.kidsatrandomhouse.co.uk/littleprincesses

Little Princesses
The Silk Princess

Katie Chase

Rosie knows a very special secret.
Hidden in her great-aunt's mysterious
Scottish castle are lots of little
princesses for her to find. And
each one will whisk her away to
another part of the world on a
magical adventure!

When Rosie finds herself in India,
the princess is missing and the
kingdom is in mourning. Then
she meets an orphan, Suvita, and
they set off to find the treasure
that Suvita's mother left her, but
can they also solve the mystery
of the missing princess?

Join Rosie and meet her exciting
new friends, as she discovers all
the Little Princesses.

978 0 099 48838 5

www.kidsatrandomhouse.co.uk/littleprincesses

Little Princesses
The Cloud Princess

Katie Chase

Rosie knows a very special secret. Hidden in her
great-aunt's mysterious Scottish castle are lots of
little princesses for her to find. And each one
will whisk her away to another part of the
world on a magical adventure!

Isadora, the Cloud Princess, is desperate for the
goddess Juventas to remove the curse that she has
put on Isadora's brother. With help from Cupid,
the God of Love, Isadora and Rosie set off for the
Garden of Heaven, but on the way, they
must escape from the evil Harpies!

Join Rosie and meet her exciting new friends,
as she discovers all the Little Princesses.

978 0 099 48835 4

www.**kidsatrandomhouse**.co.uk/littleprincesses